THE WAY WEST

JOURNAL OF A PIONEER WOMAN

THE WAY WEST

JOURNAL OF A PIONEER WOMAN

by Amelia Stewart Knight
adapted with an introduction by Lillian Schlissel
pictures by Michael McCurdy

Simon & Schuster Books for Young Readers
Published by Simon & Schuster
New York • London • Toronto • Sydney • Tokyo • Singapore

INTRODUCTION

This is the true story of Amelia Stewart Knight, her husband, and their seven children, who set out from Monroe County, Iowa, for the Oregon Territory in 1853. The boys were named Jefferson, Seneca, Plutarch, and Chatfield. The girls were Lucy, Frances, and Almira. The Knights started their journey in Iowa. Other families started in little towns along the Missouri River called jumping-off places because the travelers were leaving the United States and setting out through Indian Territory.

The overlanders traveled in big wagons pulled by yokes of six or eight oxen. Mrs. Knight cooked with "buffalo chips" over dusty fires. She rolled her pie dough on the wagon seat. If a family took their cows and dogs with them, the animals had to walk beside the wagons for more than a thousand miles.

A big wagon heavy with supplies could travel only ten or fifteen miles a day. It might take four to six months for a family to reach the Pacific coast. Only a few places existed on the long road where they could stop for repairs

or more food. When the oxen got tired, or when the road got too rough, families lightened their loads by throwing away things they loved—rocking chairs, cradles, and even a piano might be left at the side of the road.

There were many rivers to cross on the long journey. But the people were ingenious; they painted the sides of their wagons with tar to keep water out. Then they lifted the wagon right off the flatbed and floated it across the river like a boat. They piled their belongings on the wagon bed and pushed that across the river like a raft. Indians helped the overlanders, warning them against quicksand, and trading salmon, deer meat, and moccasins for cloth and money.

When the overlanders came to the mountains, the work was different. The men pulled the wagons up to the mountaintops with winches and chains, and the women and children set rocks at the back wheels to keep the wagons from sliding down. Once they got to the top, the men tied strong rope around the wagons and pulled hard to keep them from smashing on the way down the other side.

Rain soaked through the canvas covers of the wagons, and people often became ill. Children were injured climbing on and off the moving wagons, and sometimes got lost when they strayed.

Mrs. Knight does not tell you until the very end that she is expecting another baby. You must remember her secret as you read.

L.S.

SATURDAY, APRIL 9, 1853. STARTED FROM HOME about eleven o'clock and traveled eight miles and camped in an old house; night cold and frosty.

MONDAY, APRIL 11, 1853. Jefferson and Lucy have the mumps. Poor cattle bawled all night.

THURSDAY, APRIL 14, 1853. Sixteen wagons all getting ready to cross the creek. Hurrah boys, all ready. Gee up Tip and Tyler, and away we go, the sun just rising.
(evening) The men have pitched the tent and are hunting something to make a fire to get supper.

SATURDAY, APRIL 16, 1853. Made our beds down in the tent in the wet and mud. Bed clothes nearly spoiled. Cold and cloudy this morning, and everybody out of humour. Seneca is half sick. Plutarch has broke his saddle girth. Husband is scolding and hurrying all hands and Almira says she wished she was home and I say ditto. "Home, Sweet Home."

THURSDAY, APRIL 21, 1853. Rained all night; is still raining. I have just counted seventeen wagons traveling ahead of us in the mud and water. No feed for our poor stock to be got at any price. Have to feed them flour and meal.

SATURDAY, APRIL 23, 1853. Still in camp. It rained hard all night, and blew a hurricane almost. All the tents were blown down, and some wagons capsized. . . . Dreary times, wet and muddy and crowded in the tent, cold and wet and uncomfortable in the wagon. No place for the poor children.

MONDAY, MAY 2, 1853. Pleasant evening. Threw away several jars, some wooden buckets, and all our pickles. Too unhandy to carry. Indians come to our camp every day, begging money and something to eat. Children are getting used to them.

SATURDAY, MAY 7, 1853. We have crossed a small creek, with a narrow Indian bridge across it. Paid the Indians seventy-five cents toll.

SUNDAY, MAY 8, 1853. There are three hundred or more wagons in sight and as far as the eye can reach, the land is covered, on each side of the river, with cattle and horses. There is no ferry here and the men will have to make one out of the tightest wagon bed. Everything must now be hauled out of the wagons, then the wagons must be all taken to pieces, and then by means of a strong rope stretched across the river, with a tight wagon bed attached to the middle of it, the rope must be long enough to pull from one side to the other, with men on each side of the river to pull it. In this way we have to cross everything a little at a time. Women and children last, and then swim the cattle and horses. There were three horses and some cattle drowned while crossing this place yesterday.

WEDNESDAY, MAY 11, 1853. It has been very dusty yesterday and today. The men all have their false eyes (goggles) on to keep the dust out.

FRIDAY, MAY 13, 1853. It is thundering and bids fair for rain. Crossed the river very early this morning before breakfast. Got breakfast over after a fashion. Sand all around ankle deep; wind blowing; no matter, hurry it over. Them that eat the most breakfast eat the most sand.

MONDAY, MAY 16, 1853. This afternoon it rained, hailed, and the wind was very high. Have been traveling all the afternoon in mud and water up to our hubs. Broke chains and stuck in the mud several times. The men and boys are all wet and muddy.

TUESDAY, MAY 17, 1853. I never saw such a storm. The wind was so high I thought it would tear the wagons to pieces. All had to crowd into the wagons and sleep in wet beds with their wet clothes on, without supper.

MONDAY, MAY 23, 1853. The road is covered with droves of cattle and wagons—no end to them.

TUESDAY, MAY 24, 1853. Husband went back a piece this morning in search of our dog, which he found with some rascals who were trying to keep him.

SATURDAY, MAY 28, 1853. Passed a lot of men skinning a buffalo. We got a mess and cooked some of it for supper. It was very good and tender. It is the first we have seen dead or alive.

TUESDAY, MAY 31, 1853. When we started this morning there were two large droves of cattle and about fifty wagons ahead of us, and we either had to stay poking behind them in the dust or hurry up and drive past them. It was no fool of a job to be mixed up with several hundred head of cattle, and only one road to travel in, and the drovers threatening to drive their cattle over you if you attempted to

pass them. They even took out their pistols. Husband drove our team out of the road entirely, and the cattle seemed to understand it all, for they went into a trot most of the way. The rest of the boys followed with their teams and the rest of the stock. It was a rather rough ride to be sure, but was glad to get away from such a lawless set. . . . We left some swearing men behind us.

TUESDAY, JUNE 7, 1853. Just passed Fort Laramie and a large village of Sioux Indians. Numbers of them came around our wagons. Some of the women had moccasins and beads, which they wanted to trade for bread. I gave the women and children all the cakes I had baked. Husband traded a big Indian a lot of hard crackers for a pair of moccasins, [but when they] had eaten the crackers he wanted the moccasins back. We handed the moccasins to him in a hurry and drove away as soon as possible.

SATURDAY, JUNE 11, 1853. The last of the Black Hills we crossed this afternoon, over the roughest and most desolate piece of ground that was ever made (called by some the Devil's Crater). Not a drop of water, nor a spear of grass, nothing but barren hills.
—We reached Platte River about noon, and our cattle were so crazy for water that some of them plunged headlong into the river with their yokes on.

WEDNESDAY, JUNE 15, 1853. Passed Independence Rock this afternoon, and crossed Sweetwater River on a bridge. Paid three dollars a wagon and swam the stock across. The river is very high and swift. There are cattle and horses drowned there every day; there was one cow went under the bridge and was drowned, while we were crossing. The bridge is very rickety and must soon break down.

TUESDAY, JUNE 21, 1853. We have traveled over mountains close to banks of snow. Had plenty of snow water to drink. (Mr. Knight) brought me a large bucket of snow and one of our hands brought me a beautiful bunch of flowers which he said was growing close to the snow which was about six feet deep.

WEDNESDAY, JUNE 22, 1853. Very cold. Water froze over in the buckets; the boys have on their overcoats and mittens.

SUNDAY, JUNE 26, 1853. All hands come into camp tired and out of heart. Husband and myself sick. No feed for the stock. One ox lame. Camp on the bank of Big Sandy again.

MONDAY, JUNE 27, 1853. It is all hurry and bustle to get things in order. It's children milk the cows, all hands help yoke these cattle, the d---l's in them. Plutarch answers, "I can't, I must hold the tent up, it's blowing away." Hurrah boys. Who tied these horses? "Seneca, don't stand there with your hands in your pockets. Get your saddles and be ready."

WEDNESDAY, JUNE 29, 1853. The wagons are all crowded at the ferry waiting with impatience to cross. There are thirty or more to cross before us. Have to cross one at a time. Have to pay [the Indians] eight dollars for a wagon; one dollar for a horse or a cow. We swim all our stock.

SUNDAY, JULY 3, 1853. Two of our oxen are quite lame.

MONDAY, JULY 4, 1853. Chatfield has been sick all day with fever partly caused by mosquito bites.

THURSDAY, JULY 7, 1853. Our poor dog gave out with the heat so that he could not travel. The boys have gone back after him.

THURSDAY, JULY 14, 1853. It is dust from morning until night, with now and then a sprinkling of gnats and mosquitoes, and as far as the eye can reach there is nothing but a sandy desert, covered with wild sagebrush, dried up with the heat. I have ridden in the wagon and taken care of Chatfield till I got tired, then I got out and walked in the sand and through stinking sagebrush till I gave out.

SUNDAY, JULY 17, 1853. Travel over some rocky ground. Chat fell out of the wagon, but did not get hurt much.

FRIDAY, JULY 22, 1853. Here Chat had a very narrow escape from being run over. Just as we were all getting ready to start, Chatfield, the rascal, came around the forward wheel to get into the wagon, and at that moment the cattle started and he fell under the wagon. Somehow he kept from under the wheels, and escaped with only a good, or I should say, a bad scare. I never was so much frightened in my life.

SATURDAY, JULY 23, 1853. The empty wagons, cattle, and horses have to be taken further up the river and crossed by means of chains and ropes. The way we cross this branch is to climb down about six feet on the rocks, and then a wagon bed bottom will just reach across from rocks to rocks. It must then be fastened at each end with ropes or chains, so that you can cross on it, and then we climb up the rocks on the other side, and in this way everything has to be taken across. Some take their wagons to pieces and take them over in that way.

MONDAY, JULY 25, 1853. We have got on to a place in the road that is full of rattlesnakes.

THURSDAY, JULY 28, 1853. Have traveled twelve miles today and have camped in the prairie five or six miles from water. Chat is quite sick with scarlet fever.

FRIDAY, JULY 29, 1853. Chat is some better.

THURSDAY, AUGUST 4, 1853. Have seen a good many Indians and bought fish of them. They all seem peaceable and friendly.

FRIDAY, AUGUST 5, 1853. Tomorrow we will cross the Snake River. Our worst trouble at these large rivers is swimming the stock over. Often after swimming half the way over, the poor things will turn and come out again. At this place, however, there are Indians who swim the river from morning till night. There is many a drove of cattle that could not be got over without their help. By paying a small sum, they will take a horse by the bridle or halter and swim over with him. The rest of the horses all follow and the cattle will almost always follow the horses.

MONDAY, AUGUST 8, 1853. We left, unknowingly, our Lucy behind. Not a soul had missed her until we had gone some miles, when we stopped awhile to rest the cattle. Just then another train drove up behind with Lucy. She was terribly frightened and so were some more of us when we found out what a narrow escape she had run. She said she was sitting under the bank of the river when we started and did not know we were ready. And I supposed she was in Carl's wagon, as he always took charge of Frances and Lucy. . . . He supposed she was with me. It was a lesson to all of us.

FRIDAY, AUGUST 12, 1853. We were traveling slowly when one of our oxen dropped dead in the yoke. We unyoked and turned out the odd ox, and drove around the dead one. . . . I could hardly help shedding tears, and shame on the man who has no pity for the poor dumb brutes that have to travel and toil month after month on this desolate road.

WEDNESDAY, AUGUST 17, 1853. There are fifty or more wagons camped around us. Lucy and Almira have their feet and legs (covered with poison ivy).
—Bought some fresh salmon of the Indians this evening, which is quite a treat to us. It is the first we have seen.

WEDNESDAY, AUGUST 31, 1853. It is still raining this morning. The air cold and chilly. It blew so hard last night as to blow our buckets and pans from under the wagons, and this morning we found them scattered all over the valley.

THURSDAY, SEPTEMBER 1, 1853. After traveling eleven miles and ascending a long hill, we have encamped not far from the Columbia River and made a nice dinner of fried salmon. Quite a number of Indians were camped around us, for the purpose of selling salmon to the emigrants.

SATURDAY, SEPTEMBER 3, 1853. Here husband (being out of money) sold his sorrell mare (Fan) for a hundred and twenty-five dollars.

MONDAY, SEPTEMBER 5, 1853. Ascended a long steep hill this morning which was very hard on the cattle and also on myself, as I thought I never should get to the top.

FRIDAY, SEPTEMBER 9, 1853. There is a great deal of laurel growing here, which will poison the stock if they eat it. There is no end to the wagons, buggies, yokes, chains, etc., that are lying all along this road. Some splendid good wagons, just left standing, perhaps with the owners' names on them; and many are the poor horses, mules, oxen, cows, etc., that are lying dead in these mountains.

SATURDAY, SEPTEMBER 10, 1853. It would be useless for me to describe the awful road we have just passed over. . . . It is very rocky all the way, quite steep, winding, sideling, deep down, slippery and muddy . . . and this road is cut down so deep that at times the cattle and wagons are almost out of sight . . . the poor cattle all straining to hold back the heavy wagons on the slippery road.

TUESDAY, SEPTEMBER 13, 1853. We are in Oregon, with no home, except our wagons and tent.

SATURDAY, SEPTEMBER 17, 1853. A few days later my eighth child was born. We picked up and ferried across the Columbia River, utilizing skiff, canoes, and flatboat to get across, taking three days to complete. Husband traded two yoke of oxen for a half section of land with one half acre planted to potatoes, and a small log cabin and lean-to with no windows.

This is the journey's end.

In time, the hardships of the overland journey would be forgotten. Those who settled in the Oregon Territory prospered, and the Territory itself came into the Union divided into the two states of Oregon and Washington. Chatfield, Plutarch, Frances, Seneca, Jefferson, Lucy, and Almira, and the youngest one, Wilson, born on the journey itself, were among the youngest pioneers.

SIMON & SCHUSTER BOOKS FOR YOUNG READERS, Simon & Schuster Building, Rockefeller Center, 1230 Avenue of the Americas, New York, New York 10020. Text adaptation copyright © 1993 by Simon & Schuster. Illustrations copyright © 1993 by Michael McCurdy. All rights reserved including the right of reproduction in whole or in part in any form. SIMON & SCHUSTER BOOKS FOR YOUNG READERS is a trademark of Simon & Schuster. Designed by Lucille Chomowicz. The text of this book is set in 13 point Trajanus. The illustrations were done in colored scratchboard. Manufactured in the United States of America

10 9 8 7 6 5 4 3 2

Library of Congress Cataloging-in-Publication Data. Schlissel, Lillian. The way west : based on diaries of Mrs. Amelia Stewart Knight / adapted by Lillian Schlissel ; illustrated by Michael McCurdy. p. cm. Summary: An adaptation of a diary of Amelia Stewart Knight written while she, her husband, and seven children journeyed from Iowa to the Oregon Territory in 1853. 1. West (U.S.)—Description and travel—1848-1860—Juvenile literature. 2. Overland journeys to the Pacific—Juvenile literature. 3. Knight, Amelia Stewart—Diaries—Juvenile literature. 4. Pioneers—West (U.S.)—Diaries—Juvenile literature. 5. Women pioneers—West (U.S.)—Diaries—Juvenile literature. [1. Overland journeys to the Pacific. 2. Knight, Amelia Stewart. 3. Pioneers. 4. Frontier and pioneer life. 5. Diaries.] I. Knight, Amelia Stewart. II. McCurdy, Michael, ill. III. Title.
F593.S336 1993 917.804'2—dc20 92-15769 CIP   ISBN: 0-671-72375-8